Dear Parent:
Your child's love of reading starts here!

Every child learns to read in a different way and at his or her own speed. Some go back and forth between reading levels and read favorite books again and again. Others read through each level in order. You can help your young reader improve and become more confident by encouraging his or her own interests and abilities. From books your child reads with you to the first books he or she reads alone, there are I Can Read Books for every stage of reading:

SHARED READING
Basic language, word repetition, and whimsical illustrations, ideal for sharing with your emergent reader

BEGINNING READING
Short sentences, familiar words, and simple concepts for children eager to read on their own

READING WITH HELP
Engaging stories, longer sentences, and language play for developing readers

READING ALONE
Complex plots, challenging vocabulary, and high-interest topics for the independent reader

ADVANCED READING
Short paragraphs, chapters, and exciting themes for the perfect bridge to chapter books

I Can Read Books have introduced children to the joy of reading since 1957. Featuring award-winning authors and illustrators and a fabulous cast of beloved characters, I Can Read Books set the standard for beginning readers.

A lifetime of discovery begins with the magical words "I Can Read!"

Visit www.icanread.com for information
on enriching your child's reading experience.

I Can Read Book® is a trademark of HarperCollins Publishers.

Mia and the Tiny Toe Shoes
Copyright © 2012 by HarperCollins Publishers
All rights reserved. Manufactured in China.
No part of this book may be used or reproduced in any manner whatsoever without written permission except in the case of brief quotations embodied in critical articles and reviews. For information address HarperCollins Children's Books, a division of HarperCollins Publishers, 10 East 53rd Street, New York, NY 10022.
www.icanread.com
Book design by Sean Boggs
Library of Congress Catalog Card Number 2011945728
ISBN 978-0-06-208683-9 (trade bdg.) — ISBN 978-0-06-208682-2 (pbk.)

12 13 14 15 16   SCP   10 9 8 7 6 5 4 3 2 1   ❖   First Edition

Mia
and the
Tiny Toe Shoes

by Robin Farley
pictures by Aleksey and Olga Ivanov

HARPER
An Imprint of HarperCollinsPublishers

Today is a big day.
Mia is helping
the littlest dancers.

Liz wobbles back and forth.

This is hard for her.

"Now we'll try
second position," Mia says.

12

Mia takes a small step
to one side.

Kate takes a sideways hop.

Her feet are far, far apart.

"Take just a little step,"
says Mia.

She sees Kate frown.

"Last one," Mia says.
"Third position!"

Mia points one toe.
She moves the foot
in front.

Jane kicks

when she moves her foot.

"Oh my!" says Mia.

"Let's try the steps together,"
Mia tells the class.
She looks around the room.

Liz is wobbling.

Kate is hopping.

Jane is kicking.

"This is not working,"
says Mia.
How will she teach her dance?

Then Mia has an idea.

"These steps are hard," she says,

"but you are good dancers!"

Mia tells the class her plan.
Miss Bird is ready
to watch their dance.

Mia puts on music.

"First position," she calls.

Liz wobbles up front.

"Now, bend!" sings Mia.
Liz turns her wobble
into a fancy bow!

"Second position," Mia says.

Kate starts to move her feet.

"Leap!" Mia tells her.

Kate's big hop

turns into a soaring leap!

"Third position," says Mia.

The girls start to move.

"Kick!" Mia calls to Jane.

Jane kicks her leg up
super high!

"How grand!" Miss Bird cheers.
"You turned the hardest steps
into your best moves!

I'm proud of you all,"
sings Miss Bird.
Miss Bird gives everyone
a big hug.

Dictionary

Wobbling

(you say it like this: wah-bull-ing)

When a ballerina just can't keep
her legs still

Leap

(you say it like this: leep)

Taking a big jump

Soaring

(you say it like this: sor-ing)

Leaping through the air